Acknowledgments from Lanny and Bill

We would like to thank the Naples Humane Society for the wonderful programs and services they provide. In addition, we are grateful to our friends, Pat Brunn and Leni Edwards, for their assistance and encouragement.

Acknowledgments from Barlow

I wish to thank everyone who works for animal control and in the animal shelters for saving my life. I would not have survived very long in the Everglades on my own. The many volunteers who work miracles at the Naples Humane Society also have my undying gratitude. Without them, I would not have met my new, loving family. I guess even dogs have angels. I hope my story encourages others to rescue lost or forgotten pets. They will warm your hearts, make you laugh, and love you unconditionally.

This is Barlow wearing his Pet Partners bandana.
He is a registered therapy dog through Pet Partners
International. Barlow loves to visit people in hospitals
and nursing homes and show off his tricks.

The men take Barlow to a big building. Inside he sees old dogs, young dogs, big dogs, and little dogs. Each dog has its own cage. Barlow's cage has a bowl of water in it.

As Barlow plays with the children, he sees a truck come to a stop next to the playground. Two men get out and walk toward him. One man offers Barlow a bone. When Barlow takes the bone, the second man grabs him and puts him into a cage. Barlow whimpers because he does not understand why he is in a cage.

The next morning, Barlow goes back to the lake for a drink. When he is no longer thirsty, Barlow wanders down the path next to the lake. He chases a few squirrels, sniffs the grass, and takes a nap in a clump of bushes.

His growling stomach awakens him. Returning to the path, he follows it to a school. Children are playing outside on the playground. *What luck*, he thinks. Barlow shows off all his tricks hoping the delighted children will feed him.

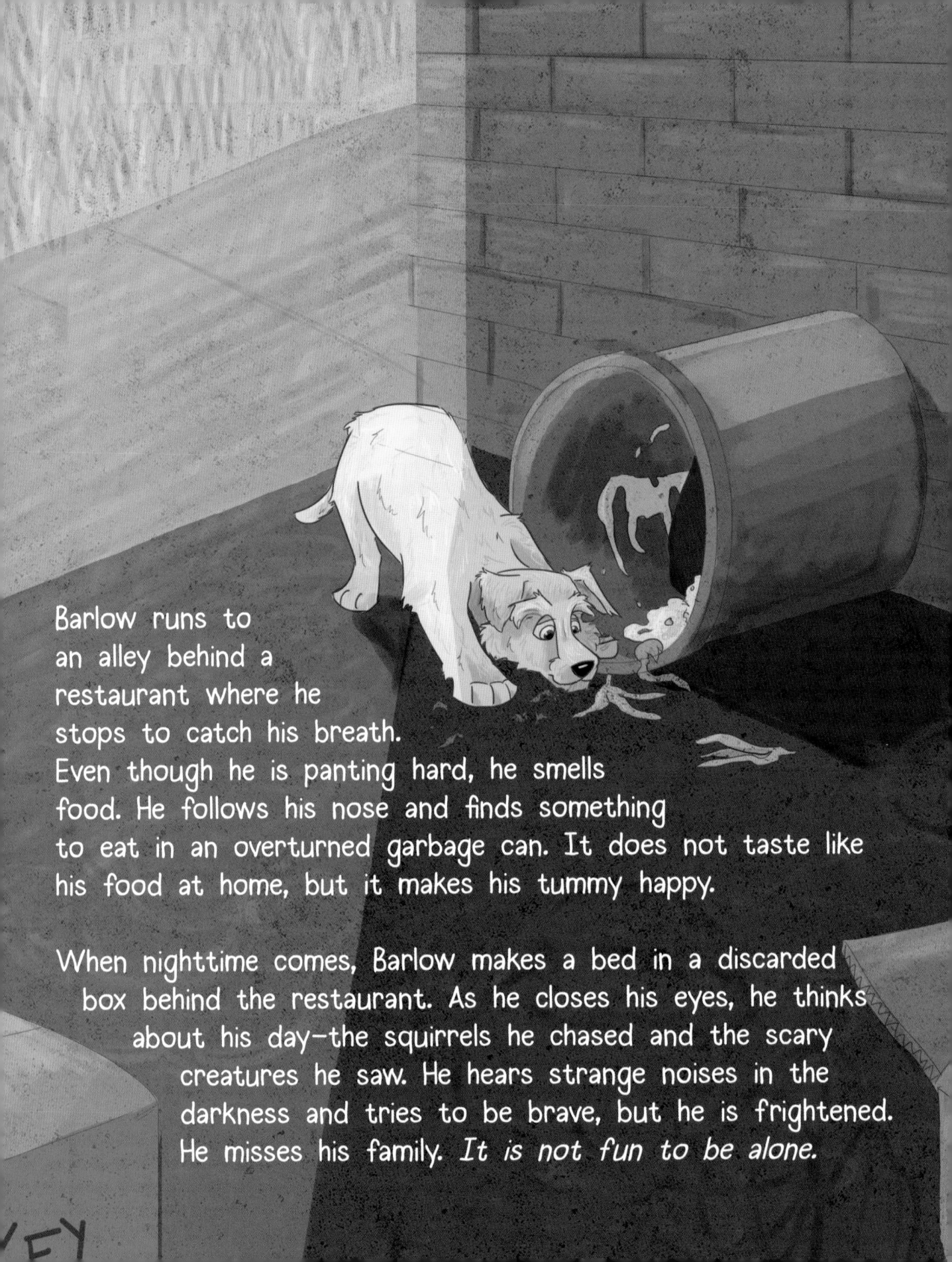

Barlow runs to
an alley behind a
restaurant where he
stops to catch his breath.
Even though he is panting hard, he smells
food. He follows his nose and finds something
to eat in an overturned garbage can. It does not taste like
his food at home, but it makes his tummy happy.

When nighttime comes, Barlow makes a bed in a discarded
box behind the restaurant. As he closes his eyes, he thinks
about his day—the squirrels he chased and the scary
creatures he saw. He hears strange noises in the
darkness and tries to be brave, but he is frightened.
He misses his family. *It is not fun to be alone.*

Barlow is hungry again. He looks for the workers who fed him the day before, but they are nowhere to be found. Hoping to find something tasty to eat, he sniffs the ground. As he searches for food, he is startled by something slithering through the weeds. It is a long, sleek creature with glassy eyes. Barlow wonders if it is hungry too. *Would it eat me?* He does not want to find out, so he scampers away.

Barlow is thirsty when he wakes up the following morning. He shakes the rainwater from his fur and trots to a nearby lake for a drink. At the lake, he sees a strange creature. It has black eyes and pointed teeth and moves silently through the water. It does not look friendly, so Barlow runs away as fast as he can.

The hours go by quickly for Barlow until the sun slides from the sky, it grows dark, and it starts to rain. Barlow does not like the rain or the dark. Shivering, he huddles under a fallen palm branch to stay dry, wishing he was back in his warm home with his family. He is alone and afraid. Worst of all, he does not even remember where his home is. Poor Barlow is lost.

After lunch, Barlow finds a playground full of children. They pet him and play with him. What a great day he is having outside!

Barlow follows the delicious smell past a lake, around a swamp, and toward a group of workers who are eating their lunches. The smell of the food makes his mouth water. He is hungry. Barlow sits at the feet of the men. He is so polite, the men share their lunches with him.

One day, Barlow notices that the front door is wide open. He can see the world beyond his house. *What is out there?* he wonders, and then darts through the opening.

Outside, Barlow feels the soft grass under his feet and the wind ruffling his fur for the first time. He hears children laughing. Best of all, a magnificent scent tickles his nose. Where is that smell coming from?

Barlow grows very fast.

He is a curious puppy who explores every corner of his house.

He sniffs things he should not sniff, eats things that are not meant to be eaten, and climbs everything he is not supposed to climb.

In a small Florida town on the edge of the Everglades swamp, three puppies are born to a proud mother and father. The parents name one of these puppies Barlow.

BARLOW,
Lost in the Everglades

William Ericksen and Lanny Scholes-Ericksen
illustrated by Alaina Hendricks